Th
Paul Bunyan

By Lori Haskins Houran

Illustrated by Luke Flowers

 A GOLDEN BOOK • NEW YORK

rhcbooks.com
Educators and librarians, for a variety of teaching tools, visit us at
RHTeachersLibrarians.com
Library of Congress Control Number: 2018959620
ISBN 978-1-9848-5179-6 (trade) — ISBN 978-1-9848-5180-2 (ebook)
Printed in the United States of America
10 9 8 7 6 5 4 3

Long ago, the pine trees in Maine grew so tall, their tops jabbed holes in the sky.

Paul Bunyan was born among those mighty pines. He was such a big baby, his parents had to use a wagon for a carriage. When he cried, his tears made puddles the size of ponds. Paul's first sneeze blew a flock of ducks south, smack in the middle of summer.

By the time he turned eighteen, Paul stood thirteen ax handles high, and he was growing an inch a day. Soon he left home to join a logging crew.

CHOP CHAMP

PAUL BUNYAN

All winter, Paul and the other lumberjacks chopped down trees. Paul worked faster than the rest of the men put together. He could fell a dozen pines with a single blow! It wasn't long before he became the boss of the crew.

Paul's first command was to the camp cook. **"More pea soup!"** he thundered. Paul was always hungry, and pea soup was his favorite.

The cook hitched up the camp wagon. He drove right across a frozen lake to the nearest town and loaded up on peas. But on the way back to camp, the wagon plunged through the ice!

Paul scratched his enormous chin.
"No problem," he said.

He poured a barrel of salt into the lake,
then a barrel of pepper. He told his men to
make a ring of logs around the edge.

Paul set the logs on fire. Soon the whole lake was boiling. The fine smell of pea soup filled the air.

"DINNER!" hollered Paul.

Winter was always cold in Maine. That year, it got so cold it snowed blue for ten days straight.

Paul was deep in the woods when he heard a whimper. It was a baby ox, shivering under a tree. The ox's white coat had turned bright blue from the snow.

"Come here, little babe," said Paul. He scooped up the ox and carried him back to camp.

Paul fed the ox a bowl of pea soup. Then he put the ox to bed in the stable.

That night, the ox began to grow. And grow . . .

The next morning, the baby ox was gone.
So was the stable.

Paul found the ox standing in the pea-soup
lake, licking the bottom dry. The stable was
perched on his back like a turtle's shell.

"Well, didn't *you* grow up fast,"
said Paul. **"But I'm still going to call
you Babe."**

Babe went to work with Paul and his crew. The first thing he did was help Paul fix the logging road. It was awfully twisty!

Paul tied one end of the road to Babe's horns. Then, with one good tug, Babe straightened that road right out.

The days kept getting colder. Raccoons stole the coats off sleeping bears. Fish grew fur over their gills. And one morning, the lumberjacks' words froze solid in midair.

"Hello! Hello!" they called. But they couldn't hear a thing. Not till spring, when the words finally thawed.

The river thawed, too. Babe helped Paul's crew push the logs into the water.

"Ride these logs down the river. Don't stop till you reach the nearest sawmill," Paul told ten of his men.

Then he and Babe headed west with the rest of the crew.

Turns out, that river didn't lead to a sawmill. It didn't lead to anything at all! It was the Round River, and it flowed around and around in a big circle.

Paul's men didn't know what to do, so they just kept right on riding the logs.

Twenty years later, Paul passed by the same spot. There were his men, with long white beards, still floating along the river. The water had worn the logs down to slender sticks!

"Might as well put those sticks to good use," said Paul. He made the sticks into fishing poles, and his men caught the last of the furry fish from the Round River. (This is why you almost never see a fish with fur anymore.)

Paul and Babe crisscrossed the country,
logging forests from Maine to California and
back again. They made some important stops
along the way. . . .

In Oregon, Paul put out a campfire by piling rocks on it. That's how Mount Hood came to be.

Across Minnesota, Paul's and Babe's footprints filled with rain. Those prints became Minnesota's famous 10,000 lakes.

And on the way through Arizona, Paul dragged his ax along the ground—and carved out the Grand Canyon!

Lumberjacks came and went, but none left
their mark like the great Paul Bunyan.

Logging Legend

Paul Bunyan wasn't a real person. He was invented by lumberjacks, who liked to tell each other wild tales. The tales got taller and taller over time—much like Paul himself!

Folks in Maine swear he was created there, but other states lay claim to him, too. You can find statues of Paul Bunyan in Maine, Michigan, Minnesota, Indiana, Wisconsin, Oregon, and California.